FM

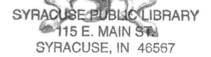

www.houghtonmifflinbooks.com

The text of this book is set in 13-point New Century Schoolbook.

Library of Congress Cataloging-in-Publication Data

Boase, Susan
Lucky Boy / by Susan Boase.
p.   cm.
Summary: A neglected dog finds a real home with a grieving widower who needs a friend.
ISBN 0-618-13175-2
[1. Dogs—Fiction. 2. Grief—Fiction.] I. Title.
PZ7.B6312 Lu 2002   [E]—dc21   2001039254

Printed in Singapore
TWP 10 9 8 7 6 5 4 3 2 1

For my mother, who taught me to read
For my father, who taught me to laugh
And for my dogs, who taught me to love unconditionally

He didn't start out lucky.

He was just Boy, as in "Here,
Boy," "Down, Boy," "Good Boy,"
"Bad Boy." How he came to be
a part of the Gustin family
was a long-lost fact. It wasn't as
if they had even wanted a dog.
He was an afterthought, a whim
someone had one day while
passing a box marked "Free" in
front of the supermarket.

The Gustins were not bad people—they just had no time for Boy. They had time for other things. Always on the go to work or school, they shopped a lot, took off on weekends, and filled their lives with things more important than the little brown dog.

Boy knew they would never let him in the house or take him for a ride in the car because he was kind of stinky; they always told him that. So he sat in the backyard, day after day, month after month. There wasn't much to look at; he had looked. One small shrub shaded a spot along the fence. A clothesline ran the length of the yard but was no longer used since the Gustins had bought a new dryer the year before. A doghouse had been hastily installed in the corner by the back porch. The yard was cold and muddy in the winter and hot and dusty in the summer.

This day it was spring, neither hot nor cold, just perfect. Boy lay on his back in the dirt, soaking up the warm sun. He kicked his stubby legs in the air. Things looked funny and new upside down, and he felt as if he could fall out of his yard and into the sky, escaping over the tall fence.

Occasionally the back door would open and someone would announce, "Here, Boy!" and set out a pan of food or water for him. He couldn't complain about the eats. If anything, the food was too plentiful and he was riding low these days. He made constitutional laps around the yard, but he couldn't work up much speed, and what was the point, anyway? Sometimes a cat or bird made its way into the yard and Boy was torn between being nice to keep a companion close and chasing it as hard and as fast as he could for some excitement.

His only other pleasure was in following the friendly voice of the mailman as he passed on his rounds. Boy would spy him through the knots in the fence boards and rush to talk in excited yelps all along the length of the fence. On the other side, the mailman would sing along...

"Oh, I went down South for to see my Sal, singin' polly wolly doodle all the day. For my Sal-ly she was a spunky gal, sing polly wolly doodle all the day. Fare thee well, fare thee well, fare thee well my fairy fay. For I'm off to Lou'siana for to see my Susy Anna, singin' polly wolly doodle all the day..."

Today, as every day, Boy reached the end of the fence, breathless, as the mailman turned the corner.

At the house next door, an old
man sat on a porch swing, staring
at the flowers his wife had planted
months before. The mailman
stopped for a moment. "Hello, Mr.
Miller. Just wanted to say how
sorry I was to hear about your loss."
Mr. Miller nodded and reached for
the cards the mailman held out
to him. "Take care, Mr. Miller," said
the mailman, and off he walked,
away down the street. Mr. Miller
opened one of the envelopes lying in
his lap. As he read, he felt a well
of sadness and a jolt of fear, too, of
an endless loneliness. He knew his
wasn't the only broken heart in the
world, but it certainly felt like it.

Spring turned to summer and
the days stretched longer. The
yard held the heat and, at its
center, the small dog, too. Boy's
one escape was to lie beneath
the yard's only shrub. From here
Boy couldn't see the dry yard,
the hot doghouse, or the Gustins'
own cool house, which he would
never be allowed to enter. Boy
paid much attention to the fence
for, behind it, he heard the old
man in the backyard. It seemed
the man spent many hours of
every day puttering and talking
in a low voice. Boy jumped as
high as he could to catch the
man's attention, but his fat little
body wouldn't float, and he fell
to the ground with a thud.
Giving up, he crawled beneath
the shrub and lay down.

The ground felt almost cool, and as Boy stood and turned in a circle
he had an urge to dig. He found that as he dug, the earth became cooler
and cooler. As the days passed and the heat grew more unbearable,
Boy dug deeper and deeper behind his shrub. He dug until his body lay
in the depression, with only his nose and eyes above the top of the
hole. From here he could see underneath the fence into the
neighbor's yard, and he watched as the old man
worked the soil in his vegetable garden. The yard
was beautiful. It was planted with thick,
flowering trees and shrubs and had an
expanse of lush, green grass.

Boy began to dig under the fence. It took hours and was the biggest effort of his life. When he finally emerged on the other side, it was dark. He had come up through a soft compost pile, which now collapsed into the tunnel he had dug. He sat damp and shivering on the soft lawn. The constellations swirled above him, and a terrifying sense of freedom swept through him. The man's house was dark and quiet. Boy found a soft flannel shirt that had been discarded on the grass. Exhausted, he curled up on it and slept through the night.

The sun found Boy stretched out on the shirt. "And what is this?" cried Mr. Miller as he leaned over the small dog. Boy awoke and looked shyly into the man's eyes. The man gazed around the yard, checking to see if the gates were still locked. He scanned the fence for a break but saw none. He even looked to the sky, as if Boy might have descended from the heavens. Then he grinned, and said, "Lord knows where you came from, but you must be in the right place, seeing as how you can't get out!" Mr. Miller picked him up and carried him into the house.

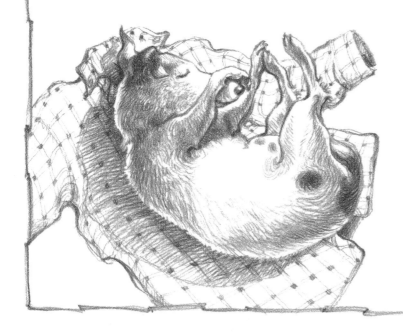

The first stop was the utility tub on the back porch, where Mr. Miller bathed and dried the little dog. "Why, I'll be!" said Mr. Miller. "You're not brown at all!" For the first time in his life, Boy felt clean. His white fur glistened and his brown spots gleamed. "Come on, I'll take you on a tour of the house...this is the kitchen, and it could use some cleaning..." he said apologetically. Boy surveyed a sunny room with scattered rag rugs on black and white linoleum. It took some getting used to, walking on that floor.

They came to the back bedroom, where Mr. Miller invited Boy to jump up on the bed. "So long as you're clean, I don't see the harm in it. Although, saints be praised, Mary would never have approved!" Boy flopped on his back and swiveled this way and that. Sounds escaped from him that he had never made before. Sounds of bliss. Mr. Miller laughed and clapped his hands. "It's been a good, long time since I've had a laugh. You and I are lucky to have found each other, Boy!" And, with that, Boy became Lucky Boy.

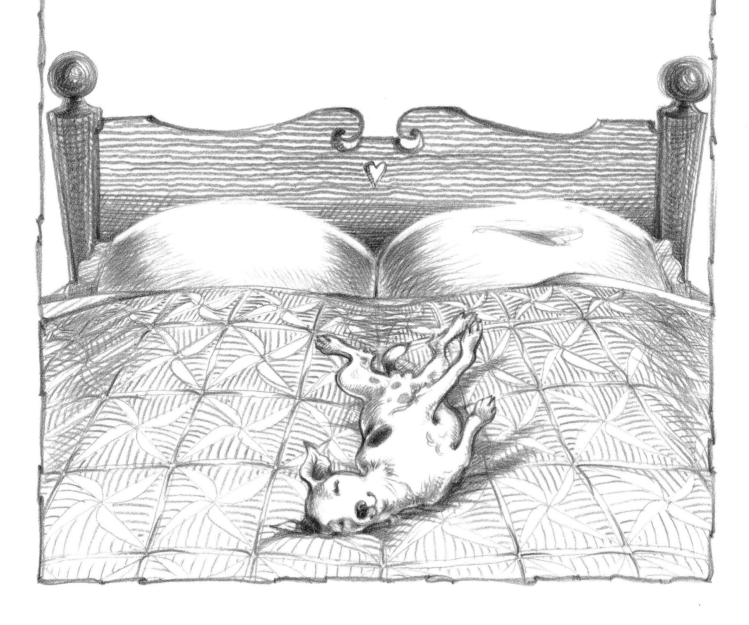

Mr. Miller scanned the cupboard and refrigerator shelves and came to the conclusion that he had no food suitable for a dog. He had hardly any food suitable for a human, for that matter. "Guess I've kind of let things go around here, Lucky Boy. Don't know what I *have* been eating!" And so they set off for the store.

Lucky Boy sat in the front with the window rolled down so he could catch the breeze. Oh, to go so fast that things became a blur! To feel the wind course through his nose till he couldn't breathe, and to sneeze the biggest sneeze of his life! Mr. Miller laughed and laughed until he had to pull off to the side of the road.

Lucky Boy waited in the car with the windows rolled down while
Mr. Miller went into the store to buy groceries, a collar, and a leash.
People passing the car commented, "What a cute dog!" "Why, he
looks just like he's driving!" "My, how well behaved he is!" Lucky
Boy's tail sounded a rhythmic beat all the way home.

Back home, as Mr. Miller prepared breakfast, the kitchen filled with heavenly smells of bacon and eggs, toast, and coffee. Offering little bits of this and that to Lucky Boy, Mr. Miller said, "I don't know why I feel so sneaky. It's not as if anyone is here to tell on us." Lucky Boy wagged his tail and looked into Mr. Miller's eyes. "Lucky Boy, you don't have any idea what I'm talking about, but it feels so good to talk to someone." Lucky Boy's tail wagged so hard that he slid about on the linoleum floor. Mr. Miller set a bowl of eggs and bacon on the floor. "Eat up!" he said.

After breakfast, Mr. Miller put the new collar around Lucky Boy's neck and attached the leash. They walked along the sidewalk, and Lucky Boy shook from head to tail in a little freedom dance. "Lucky Boy," said Mr. Miller, laughing, "you make me very happy!"

As they approached the house on the corner,
the Gustin family emerged in a rush.

"Hey!" whispered the oldest child to his parents, "that looks like our dog over there, only our dog was brown." Mrs. Gustin looked guiltily over at Mr. Gustin. Their little brown dog had disappeared—they weren't sure when, and they hadn't even bothered to look for him. They had, to tell the truth, considered his disappearance a blessing. He had been just one more thing to take care of in their busy lives. "Yes, well..." said Mrs. Gustin. And with that, they piled into their car.

Mr. Miller and Lucky Boy stood at a distance and watched them zoom away. "Those are the busiest folks I *ever* did see!" said Mr. Miller. The dog cocked his head, and Mr. Miller could swear he smiled. "So, little buddy, how about that walk?" Off they went, noticing all the plants in bloom, saying hello to neighbors and strangers alike. People stopped them to strike up conversations. They met all the dogs and cats in the neighborhood and took note of each and every fire hydrant, bush, tree, and pole along the way.

And after their walk, while Mr. Miller and Lucky Boy rested, the mailman rounded the corner. Mr. Miller smiled in greeting, Lucky Boy cocked his head, and the mailman gave the happy little dog a big wink. "Beautiful day, eh?" he said, and off on his rounds he went, singing, *"Oh, I went down South for to see my Sal, singin' polly wolly doodle all the day..."*